Adventure According to Humphrey

I heard voices.

'Can't I carry it?' Richie begged.

'Better if I do it,' Kirk replied.

It took me a few sleepy moments to realize that I was still in the tall ship, which the boys were carrying to the bus for the trip to Potter's Pond! I was about to squeak up in protest, when I realized that, at last, I had my one chance for real adventure.

Betty G. Birney has written episodes for many children's television shows and is the author of over twenty-five picture books. Her work has won many awards, including an Emmy and three Humanitas Prizes. She lives with her family in America.

Specially published for World
Book Day 2008

Join Humphrey on more of his adventures!

・ö・

The World According to Humphrey
Friendship According to Humphrey

Coming soon:
Trouble According to Humphrey

・ö・

Praise for *The World According to Humphrey*:

'Humphrey, a delightful, irresistible character, is big hearted, observant and creative, and his experiences . . . range from comedic to touching.' *Booklist*

'This read is simply good-good-good.' *Kirkus Reviews*

'Breezy, well-crafted first novel.' *Publishers Weekly*

・ö・

Praise for *Friendship According to Humphrey*:

'An effective exploration of the joys and pains of making and keeping friends, which will strike a chord with many children.' *Daily Telegraph*

Adventure According to Humphrey

Betty G. Birney

Special Publication for World
Book Day 2008

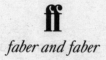

faber and faber

First published by
Faber and Faber Limited in 2008
For World Book Day 2008
3 Queen Square London WC1N 3AU

Typeset by Faber and Faber
Printed in the UK by CPI Bookmarque, Croydon, CR0 4TD

A CIP record for this book
is available from the British Library

ISBN 978–0–571–23862–0

2 4 6 8 10 9 7 5 3 1

To Humphrey's GREAT-GREAT-GREAT fans
and friends in the UK

Contents

Class Ahoy!

'Guess what *I* did this weekend!' Heidi blurted out one sunny Monday morning.

As usual, my friends in Room 26 of Longfellow School had returned to class with wonderful stories about what they'd done over the weekend.

'Raise-Your-Hand-Heidi, please,' said Mrs Brisbane. She always reminded Heidi to raise her hand, but sometimes Heidi still forgot.

When she raised her hand, Mrs Brisbane asked, 'Okay, what *did* you do this weekend?'

'We went on a hike to a cave and waded through an underground stream,' Heidi proudly explained.

'Sounds like quite an adventure.' Then Mrs Brisbane noticed all the other hands waving in the air. 'It looks as if a lot of you had adventures.'

Oh yes, they had! Lower-Your-Voice-A.J. and Wait-for-the-Bell-Garth had gone to a cricket match. Miranda Golden (whom I think of as Golden-Miranda because she's an almost perfect human) went to the zoo. Sit-Still-Seth had gone horse riding.

'I had Humphrey at *my* house,' I-Heard-That-Kirk-Chen proudly announced.

It was true. I'd had a very pleasant weekend at Kirk's. I got to watch the telly and listen to people talk. But whenever they did something really FUN-FUN-FUN, like going to the shops or riding bikes, they left me at home.

I understand that small furry creatures like me don't normally do things like that, but as a classroom hamster who goes home with a different student each weekend, I must admit I sometimes feel a little left out. After all, I'm always ready to help my friends (or even my teacher or headmaster) solve a problem. It would be nice to share in their adventures, too.

I'm luckier than Og the frog, who is the other classroom pet. He doesn't need to be fed as often as I do and often spends weekends alone in Room 26.

While I was thinking about my friends' adventures, I lost track of what was happening in class for a moment. Mrs Brisbane was giving us our new vocabulary words for the week – and, oh, what words they were! Beautiful words like 'nautical', 'treasure' and 'squall', which Mrs Brisbane said was a violent gust of wind. They were the best vocabulary words I'd heard since I started school back in September, and I quickly jotted them down in the tiny notebook I keep hidden behind the mirror in my cage. Ms Mac, the teacher who brought me to Room 26, gave it to me before she moved to far-off Brazil. No one else knew I had it. No one knew that I had learned to read and write, either.

My fellow classmates enjoyed the vocabulary words, too. Kirk, the class clown, made a funny, angry face and said, 'Squall! Squall!' which made Stop-Giggling-Gail Morgenstern giggle. (Just about everything makes her laugh.)

The words reminded me of a pirate movie we watched at Kirk's house. Some of the pirates were SCARY-SCARY-SCARY, but it was exciting to see the big ships with their sails flapping in the wind. How I'd love to feel the sea breeze ruffling through my fur! And to hear the pirates saying things like 'Avast, matey' and 'Land ho!' I'm not sure what those things mean but they sound thrilling!

To top it all off, there was treasure buried on an island. I sometimes hide food to save for the future, but the pirates hid gold and silver and shiny jewels.

I already have many adventures of my own, especially when I escape from my cage, which I can do easily because it has a lock-that-doesn't-lock. It looks firmly closed, but I can jiggle it open, get out of my cage to help my friends and return without anyone knowing it. Most of my exploits have been in houses, flats or in Room 26, but now that it was spring, I was longing for bigger adventures.

After lunch, Mrs Brisbane began reading a book about a boy and a girl who are sent to spend the summer with their mysterious Uncle J.R. You can imagine their surprise – and mine – when he turned out to be a pirate called Jolly Roger who taught them to be pirates, too! It was called *Jolly Roger's Guide to Life*. My fur tingled and I was hanging on every word when Mrs Brisbane suddenly closed the book.

The other students groaned and I was unsqueakably disappointed, until Mrs Brisbane said she had a big announcement to make.

'Tomorrow, we'll start a project about sailing,' she said. 'We'll be doing sailing problems in maths, learning sailing terms in vocabulary and then you'll start building your own model sailing boats. Two weeks from tomorrow, if the weather is good, we'll go to Potter's Pond for a contest to see which sailing boat can get across the water first. We'll have a picnic and prizes and maybe –' Mrs Brisbane paused. 'Hidden treasure!'

Potter's Pond. Picnic. Prizes. Treasure! My heart

pounded at the possibilities and my classmates' cheers were almost deafening.

'What are the prizes?' Heidi asked.

'Raise-Your-Hand-Heidi,' Mrs Brisbane answered. 'The prizes will be a surprise.'

My friends groaned again and I let out a bit of a squeak myself.

By afternoon, Mrs Brisbane had written the rules for the sailing boat contest on the blackboard:

1 Each student will work with a partner.
2 The boat must be powered by the wind; no batteries or remote controls can be used.
3 All students will be given the same materials for their boats, but they will be allowed to add one item of their choosing (except batteries).
4 Materials will include wood, cardboard, cloth, paint, glue, markers and other art supplies.
5 There will be a prize for Most Beautiful Boat. The first boat to make it from the starting point to the opposite shore of Potter's Pond will win the prize for Most Seaworthy.

At the end of the day, my friends were still chattering away about sailing boats as they rushed out of class. Soon, Og and I had Room 26 all to ourselves.

Once the coast was clear, I shouted to my neighbour, 'Og? Did you hear all that?'

'BOING-BOING!' he replied, in the odd twangy

noise that green frogs like him make. Then he leaped into the water side of his tank. While he was splishing and splashing, I daydreamed about the pirate life. I was so deep in thought, I didn't realize that it was night time until the door flew open, the lights came on and a familiar voice said, 'Give a cheer, 'cause Aldo's here!'

'Greetings, Aldo! Did you hear about our wonderful contest?' I replied, though as usual all that came out was SQUEAK-SQUEAK-SQUEAK.

He didn't quite understand me, but as he cleaned the room, he noticed the vocabulary words on one blackboard and the rules for the contest on the other.

'So that's what you were worked up about, Humphrey!' he said with a hearty laugh. 'I'd sure like to be part of that!'

'Me, too!' I answered, and Og splashed wildly.

'In fact, I have a great idea!' Aldo announced.

I waited breathlessly for him to tell me more. Instead, he started sweeping up the aisles of the classroom. Occasionally, I'd hear him say, 'Aye-aye!' or 'Shiver me timbers,' but other than that, I had no idea what he was thinking.

When I couldn't stand it any longer, I squeaked, 'What's your idea, Aldo?'

He turned around and faced my cage. 'I know ye'd like me to tell ye, me hearty. But some things be best kept secret.'

Aldo sounded so much like a real pirate, I decided not to squeak back. It's not a good idea to argue with a pirate.

But I did wish he'd told me his idea.

Don't be asking too many questions, me hearties. Ye might not like the answers!

from *Jolly Roger's Guide to Life* by I.C. Waters

2

Learning the Ropes

BOATS-BOATS-BOATS! Just about all we talked about in Room 26 had to do with boats. There were maths problems about boats. (One had to do with a boat race.) There was a science lesson about what floats and what doesn't. (Corks float. Rocks don't.) There was a history lesson about the Vikings, and those lovely vocabulary words.

And then there was the STORY. Every day, Mrs Brisbane read another exciting chapter from the book. Imagine living on a real live pirate ship!

In just a few short days, I went from never thinking about boats to thinking about them all the time. There were so many kinds of wonderful boats, from rowing boats you move with oars and muscles to sailing boats and tall ships powered by the wind. Then there were motorboats, yachts, tugboats and ferries, which all have engines. And the great ships powered by steam. Mrs Brisbane brought in a stack of books about boats and put up huge posters on the wall.

It would be hard to choose a favourite, but the Chinese junk did catch my eye. That boat isn't junk at all, but a beautiful craft with colourful sails. I could almost feel the sea breeze tickle my whiskers whenever I looked at the picture.

In the evenings, I tried to talk to Og about boats and pirates and treasure, but as soon as I'd bring up the subject, he'd dive into his tank and swim around. Maybe he was trying to tell me that he didn't need a boat to make his way through the water.

I was a little jealous, although I still wouldn't want to be a frog. As nice as Og is, he has googly eyes, green skin and no nice soft fur at all! Most of the time, I feel a little sorry for my neighbour, except when he is swimming.

I occupied my spare time by drawing pictures of boats in my little notebook. I must admit, my drawing of the S.S. *Golden Hamster*, complete with a hamster flag, was quite impressive.

On Thursday, the class had a BIG-BIG-BIG surprise. Mrs Brisbane's husband, Bert, came to school with her, and Stop-Giggling-Gail Morgenstern's mother also arrived first thing in the morning.

'Class, I brought in some friends to help you construct your boats,' she said. 'Mr Brisbane can advise you on building them, and Mrs Morgenstern is an artist who can help you make your boats look good.'

That news created quite a stir in class. Personally, if I were sailing, I'd want a solid, seaworthy boat. But I also liked the idea of a good-looking craft. I thought having these two helpers was just the kind of idea a very clever hamster might have come up with!

However, much as I loved boats, the next afternoon I felt a little sleepy from drawing them all night, so I crawled into my sleeping hut for a doze. I woke up to the sounds of Mr Brisbane talking. 'A boat that floats is a success,' he said. 'A boat that sinks is not.'

I nodded my head in agreement and then drifted back to sleep. I was awakened again by the sound of Mrs Morgenstern's voice. 'A thing of beauty is a joy for ever,' she said. 'And your job is to make your boat a joyful reflection of who you are!'

Suddenly, I was wide awake. The S.S. *Golden Hamster* was definitely a joyful reflection of who I was. But would a boat like that actually float?

Next, my friends paired up and were soon busy making plans. If only I had a partner to help me build my boat!

'Og, would you like to build a boat with me?' I asked.

'BOING-BOING!' he answered, followed by a splashing sound.

That didn't sound like a 'yes' to me. I guess the idea of a boat is pretty silly to a creature that can swim like Og.

So I watched my fellow classmates make their plans. Mr Brisbane provided each group with a light wooden hull (the body of the boat) that he had hollowed out, because Mrs Brisbane said it was too dangerous for her students to be carving with knives. He wheeled his chair from table to table, encouraging my friends about their ideas. (Mr Brisbane moves around in a wheelchair after an accident last year, but it hasn't slowed him down one bit.)

Mrs Morgenstern also moved around to each group. She was a colourful person, wearing a red and gold flowered tunic, gold tights and high red boots. Her long hair was pulled back in a braid that went half-way down her back.

'Colour is the key!' she told Seth and Tabitha. 'Choose your colours carefully.'

'The sail's the thing,' Mr Brisbane told Art and Mandy. 'Remember, that's what powers your boat. The Vikings were great sailors. Good choice.'

Vikings! My whiskers wiggled with excitement

and I wished I could see their drawing.

Mrs Morgenstern moved to the table where her daughter, Stop-Giggling-Gail, was working with her best friend, Heidi. 'Come on, Gail,' she said. 'You can be more creative than that! Think colour!'

Gail, who was usually cheerful, wasn't even smiling. In fact, just looking at her made me feel bad, so I decided to check on my other friends.

Kirk, who was almost always joking, was very serious as he worked on his boat with his friend, Richie Rinaldi.

'I've got a great idea,' Kirk said as he quickly sketched a drawing. 'I know all about boats. We'll make it a tall ship . . . like this!'

My heart thumped a little faster. Tall ships were amazing with MANY-MANY-MANY sails billowing in the wind!

'That's cool.' Richie picked up his pencil. 'What if we put a thing on the front? A whatchamacallit?'

He started to draw on the paper but Kirk reached out and stopped Richie's hand. 'A figurehead? I don't want to take the chance. It might throw it off balance and sink the ship.' Richie stopped drawing but he didn't look very happy.

'It would look good,' he complained.

'Yep,' Kirk agreed. 'But you want to *win*, right?'

'Sure,' Richie said, although he didn't sound completely convinced.

Just then, Mr Brisbane came to their table. 'That's a fine-looking ship, boys,' he praised them. 'Good work.'

Kirk beamed with pride. Richie didn't.

Then Mrs Morgenstern's voice rang out. 'Now that's what I call colourful!' I heard her say. She was standing by the table where Sayeh and Miranda were working. 'Gail? Heidi? Look at this! Marvellous, simply marvellous.'

Heidi and Gail came over to look at the drawing.

'It's a swan boat,' Miranda explained. She sounded very proud. Speak-Up-Sayeh didn't talk a lot, but she looked proud, too.

'Okay,' said Heidi. 'We'll make ours really pretty. Right, Gail?'

Gail didn't answer. She just followed her friend back to the table and stared down at her drawing.

Seeing how unhappy Richie and Gail were, I wasn't sorry when boat-designing time was over. After Mr Brisbane and Mrs Morgenstern left, Mrs Brisbane pulled her chair to the front of the room, took out her book and began to read. The very thought of living with a real pirate gave me the shivers. But it was the good kind of shivers, where you feel happy and scared all at the same time.

When Mrs Brisbane stopped reading, my friends all begged for more. 'I'd like to read another chapter,' she said. 'But I don't think there's time'

Just then, the bell rang, announcing the end of school. The day had gone by so quickly, none of us had noticed. Not even Wait-for-the-Bell-Garth Tugwell, who was always the first one out of the door.

⚬

'Do you like the story, Og?' I asked my friend once we were alone.

He was splishing and splashing so loudly, he probably couldn't even hear me.

'I said, do you like the story?'

Og didn't answer, which was RUDE-RUDE-RUDE of him. 'Scurvy dog,' I muttered. (Well, it was more of a squeak than a mutter.) I didn't really mean it, but Uncle Jolly Roger said it all the time. It felt good to talk like a pirate!

I dozed for a while, then woke up when I heard a voice say, 'Ahoy there, me hearties!' I peeked out of my sleeping hut, half expecting to see a real pirate with a patch over his eye and a sack full of doubloons (though I wasn't quite sure what those were). Instead, I saw my old pal, Aldo, staring into my cage.

'Are ye in there, matey?' he asked.

'YES-YES-YES, and you certainly fooled me,' I squeaked.

When he threw back his head and laughed, his

moustache shook so hard I thought it might fall off. But let me tell you, Aldo's moustache is *firmly* attached. 'Ye be all right, Jack,' he replied, even though he knows my name is Humphrey.

'And don't ye be worrying – I'm not a real pirate,' he added with a wink. '*Not yet*, anyway.'

That comment got my whiskers wiggling, I can tell you! Did he mean he might become a pirate some day?

He didn't explain himself, because he was busy cleaning Room 26, as he did every night. The only sound I heard was Aldo whistling a merry tune I'd never heard before. After he cleaned the floor and emptied the waste baskets, he stood in front of my cage and said, 'Check this out.'

He began to whistle while he danced a very happy, bouncy kind of dance. When he was finished, he bowed and said, 'That's a hornpipe dance. It's named after a musical instrument sailors play. What do you think, Humphrey?'

I was happy he remembered my name again, and even happier to be able to squeak the truth. 'It was GREAT-GREAT-GREAT!'

'Thanks, matey. Gotta set sail now.' With that, he pushed his cleaning trolley out of Room 26.

It was very quiet once he was gone. So quiet, that I couldn't help remembering the thing he'd said about not being a pirate *yet*. Since Aldo was one of the nicest people I'd ever met, it was hard to think of him as a person who would steal people's treasure. Still, with his fine moustache and excellent hornpipe dancing, he might have what it takes to be a real pirate.

With humans, you never know.

> When the going gets rough, dance ye a hornpipe.
>
> from *Jolly Roger's Guide to Life* by I.C. Waters

3

Ready About

By the time class started the next morning, my mind was spinning as fast as my hamster wheel, just thinking about pirates, sailing boats and the sailing contest.

Once class began, however, there was too much going on to think about any of those things. The vocabulary test came first. I'd had boats on my mind all right, but not spelling. I took the test with my friends (sneaking into my sleeping hut to write in my notebook) and I managed to miss three words, including 'squall'. For some reason, I thought there was a 'w' in there. Like 'sprawl'. Or 'bawl'.

Next came maths. I had a little doze during that period. As soon as that was finished, Mr Brisbane and Mrs Morgenstern returned and the boat building was in full swing again. I perched near the top of my cage and watched my friends at work.

Oh, what lovely boats I saw! The boat Miranda and Sayeh were building really looked like a graceful swan. A.J. and Garth worked on a sailing boat that had a skull and crossbones pirate flag (which is called the Jolly Roger). Tabitha and Seth were building a Chinese junk – good for them! And the Viking ship designed by Art and Mandy was taking shape.

But the sailing boat to end all sailing boats was the one that Kirk and Richie were building. I should say the boat Kirk was building, because he was doing all the work. Richie, who was usually a happy-go-lucky guy, looked grumpier than I'd ever seen him before.

'Let me help,' Richie said, as Kirk sanded the hull.

'You want to win, right?' asked Kirk.

Richie nodded. 'Sure.'

'Then let me do this. I can practically promise we'll win, because I know just what to do,' Kirk assured his partner. 'My dad and I built one last year.'

'Well, I can at least *sand* it,' Richie protested but Kirk didn't give in.

'I'll do it,' he said. 'And we'll get the prize.'

Gail still wasn't enjoying the assignment any more than Richie. She and Heidi had divided the work in half. Heidi was putting together the boat while Gail was supposed to design the sail. Mrs Morgenstern seemed to love Heidi's ideas. 'Oh, those squiggles look like waves! That's a wonderful theme for the boat,' she exclaimed. Then she turned to her daughter. 'Gail, why don't you do something like that for the sails?'

Without so much as a smile, Gail said, 'I don't know.'

Mrs Morgenstern didn't seem to hear her. 'Think mermaids! Think seagulls! Think light-houses!'

I don't believe Gail was thinking about any of those things. Luckily, Mandy had a question for Mrs Morgenstern, who moved away from the table.

'Why don't you listen to your mum?' Heidi asked Gail. 'If you do what she says, maybe we'll win the prize for Most Beautiful Boat.'

Gail stared at the big poster of a sailing boat. 'See that picture on the wall?' she asked Heidi at last.

'Sure,' Heidi answered.

'What does it look like?'

Heidi thought for a moment. 'Well, it's a wooden boat with big white sails.'

Gail nodded. 'And doesn't it look beautiful sail-ing across the water with those white sails against the blue sky?'

'I guess so,' Heidi said.

'I don't think there's anything more beautiful than a sailing boat with white sails,' Gail explained. 'I hate to mess it up with mermaids and seagulls.'

'But the contest . . .' Heidi protested.

Gail sighed. 'Okay,' she said. 'I'll try.'

She sure didn't sound happy about it.

At the end of the day, after Mr Brisbane and Mrs Morgenstern left, Mrs Brisbane made a surprising – even shocking – announcement.

'Class, we were so busy with our boats this week, I forgot to arrange for anyone to take Humphrey home for the weekend.'

Whew – that statement took the wind out of my sails! For one thing, my classmates usually *begged* to take me home. For another thing, if nobody took me home, I'd get awfully hungry and thirsty because I can't go without food and water the way Og can.

Luckily, Mrs Brisbane wasn't finished. 'So I'll be taking him home with me.'

I felt a lot better hearing that. But I felt a lot worse when she said, 'And I'm afraid there's no time for me to read aloud today. We'll continue with our book on Monday.'

No time to read aloud! I was about to squeak up in protest when the bell rang. Class was over, the school day was over and as soon as Mrs Brisbane gathered up her jacket and books, we were on our way out of Room 26 for the weekend.

'Farewell, mate,' I called to Og.

'BOING-BOING!' he twanged in return. I wonder if that's how frogs say, 'Aye-aye.'

Everyone in Room 26 had been so involved with boats, I was relieved to be at the Brisbanes' house, because they always paid a lot of attention to me. So you can imagine my surprise when they continued to think of nothing but boats all weekend, too!

Mr Brisbane read about model sailing boats, sketched them and worked on them in his garage workshop. Meanwhile, Mrs Brisbane kept busy writing things on a big piece of paper. Every once in a while, she'd stop and chuckle.

When I first met Mrs Brisbane, she never chuckled. In fact, she didn't laugh at all, because Mr Brisbane had been in a car accident. But slowly, over time, she regained her sense of humour (maybe I helped just a little bit). Still, it was unusual for her to sit and chuckle in a room all by herself. Sure, I was there, too, but people often say and do very strange things in front of me, almost as if I'm invisible.

Finally, Mr Brisbane came in from the garage.

'You're still working on those lists?' he asked.

'Yes,' she said, chuckling again. 'I tell you, this is going to be one fun party.'

So that was it. She was planning the picnic at Potter's Pond. Oh, what I would give to get a peek at her list! Luckily, the Brisbanes started yawning early and even though I wished they had set up a nice obstacle course for me to run, I wasn't that sorry to see them go to bed early.

You see, I had a Plan. And when a hamster has a Plan, nothing (well, almost nothing) can stand in his way.

I waited until the house was VERY-VERY-VERY quiet. Then I fiddled with my cage door and as usual, it swung right open. Thank goodness for my lock-that-doesn't-lock!

My cage is a very nice place for snoozing and for working out on my exercise wheel and climbing equipment. It has a special corner for my poo, which I keep separate from the rest of the cage (of course!). And it has nice soft bedding, which is good for sleeping and for saving up food.

It's also a place to keep me safe from toddlers who like to poke their fingers at small creatures, and from more dangerous animals, such as dogs and cats.

But every once in a while, I love to break free and get out in the open, despite the dangers. I was feeling especially adventurous that night. Besides, the only peril I faced at the Brisbanes' house was the possibility of being caught outside my cage and having it firmly locked for ever. I was willing to take the chance, because I had a mission: to find out more about the picnic at Potter's Pond.

I could see the list was sitting right on Mrs Brisbane's desk. Of course, before I set out I had to map out my route, just like sailors and even pirates do.

I slid down the leg of the low table where my cage sat and scurried across the carpet. It felt nice on my paws, but I couldn't move as fast on it as I can on Aldo's shiny, slippery floors. The desk looked like a mountain to a small hamster like me. However, I knew that where there's a will (and a Plan), there's a way.

When I got close to the desk, I noticed a nice cosy chair with a striped blanket draped over it. I grabbed onto the blanket and pulled myself up, paw over paw, then hopped onto the desk. There was Mrs Brisbane's list, right in front of me.

In the classroom, it's easy for me to read the blackboard, where things are nice and big, but it's much harder to read a book or a piece of paper, where the letters are at an angle that's hard for a small creature to read. I've found that if I stand up on my tippy toes, I can make out at least some words.

However, when I got to the paper, I saw that Mrs Brisbane had a large rock (I think humans call it a paperweight) right on top of the list, blocking part of the writing. I could only make out a few words:

sure maps
Captain Ki
blue, red, gold

My heart was pounding. 'Sure maps' grabbed my attention. Could they be 'treasure maps?' Did Mrs Brisbane have a map leading to a chest of sparkling blue, red and gold jewels?

Captain Ki sounded like a pirate. Captain Kitty? Captain Kiwi? Was a pirate coming to the picnic?

I tried moving the paper around so I could read the rest of the words, but it wouldn't budge. I pushed the rock with all my might, but I couldn't move it an inch. I was still struggling with it when I heard Mrs Brisbane talking. Goodness, I was sure she'd been asleep for a long time!

I quickly dived off the desk and slid down the chair cover, which was like a bumpy playground slide. I landed on the seat, paused to catch my breath, then continued to slide down the leg of the chair. Next, I scurried across the floor to the table. I was moving fast, but I skidded to a stop when I realized I had no idea how to get back up. I certainly couldn't slide *up* the table leg. Still, I'm a clever hamster, so I stayed calm and checked out the area.

I breathed a sigh of relief when I discovered a big stack of magazines on the floor. Each magazine was like a step on a staircase, so I carefully climbed up them one by one. However, when I made the leap to the table, my back paws pushed the top magazine off and the whole stack collapsed. It didn't make a loud noise, but it did make noise, so I dashed into my cage and pulled the door behind me.

A few seconds later, Mrs Brisbane came shuffling out of the bedroom, wearing her dressing gown and slippers. 'I'll check it out, Bert. I'm sure it's nothing.'

She turned on the light and looked around the living room. 'Sorry to wake you, Humphrey,' she said while I tried to look as innocent as possible. Then she saw the heap of magazines. 'Oh, that's what it was,' she said, shaking her head. 'I hope they didn't scare you.'

'Just a little,' I squeaked, even though I knew she couldn't understand me.

'I'll straighten these up tomorrow,' she said, turning off the light. As she was close to the bedroom door, I heard her tell Bert, 'You're going to have to build me a magazine rack.'

'I'll be happy to,' he replied. 'After the boat race.'

It was quiet for the rest of the night but I didn't sleep a wink because of what I'd seen on Mrs Brisbane's list.

The boat race at Potter's Pond, the maps and the colourful treasure certainly sounded exciting. With a pirate on hand, it could be scary and even dangerous. Still, the more I thought about it, the more I knew that, scary or not, I didn't want to miss that boat race for anything in the world!

Listen up, maties. A map can be a pirate's best friend, unless some bilge rat has a map of his own . . . and beats ye to the treasure!

from *Jolly Roger's Guide to Life* by I.C. Waters

4

Batten Down the Hatches

I slept in late on Sunday and awoke revived and refreshed. The Brisbanes were in a happy mood and so was I. After all, I was going on a treasure hunt soon – or so I thought.

In the afternoon, Mr Brisbane brought a model sailing boat into the living room – a fine-looking craft with a crisp yellow sail and a bright red hull.

'I couldn't resist making a boat of my own,' he told Mrs Brisbane.

'It's great, but only a student can win the prize,' she replied.

'I know,' Bert said. He sat the boat on the table and opened my cage door. 'Let's see what kind of a sailor Humphrey would make,' he said.

Mrs Brisbane quickly stacked up books around the edge of the table so I couldn't escape. 'I don't think he'll like it one bit,' she said.

I couldn't believe that my teacher, who is SMART-SMART-SMART most of the time, could be so wrong! I'd make an incredible sailor – I just knew it.

Mr Brisbane gently set me in the boat. 'See, Humphrey? It's just your size.'

Yes, it was *exactly* my size. I felt as if I'd been born to sail in that boat. I stood at the bow (that's the front of the ship) and imagined myself setting sail for a far-off island in search of hidden treasure.

'Looks like he's a born sailor,' Mr Brisbane observed. Now there's a smart man!

'Don't be ridiculous,' his wife said. 'I wouldn't let Humphrey get within sight of the water.'

What an unsqueakable thing to say!

'Why?' Mr Brisbane asked.

'WHY-WHY-WHY?' I asked, too.

'Because hamsters must never get wet,' Mrs Brisbane explained. 'They'll catch a chill and get sick or even die, and water removes the good oils in a hamster's fur. You really should read up on hamsters the way I have, Bert.'

My heart sank to the bottom of my paws.

'Guess you're not going to Potter's Pond, my friend,' Mr Brisbane told me.

I felt like I was spinning without my wheel. I felt sick with disappointment. I felt just about as bad as I did when Ms Mac left and broke my hamster heart.

'No way,' Mrs Brisbane agreed. 'Besides, the poor thing would be terrified.'

A lot she knew! She had no idea of the fur-raising adventures I'd had. And I'd hardly ever been terrified, except by large and unfriendly animals, such as dogs.

Mr Brisbane put me back in my cage.

'Sorry, Humphrey,' he said.

'You think you're sorry,' I squeaked. 'I'm about the sorriest creature in the world.'

They laughed at my squeaking, which hurt my feelings, but I forgave them.

They're only humans, after all.

·ö·

Once I was back in Room 26, I spent a lot of time in my sleeping hut, trying hard not to think about boats. Every once in a while, though, I couldn't resist checking up on my friends' progress.

With Mr Brisbane's advice and help, holes were drilled, keels were attached, boats were sanded and painted, sails were raised. He seemed especially pleased with the progress Kirk and Richie were making with their tall ship. 'Just make sure that all those sails don't weigh the boat down,' he told them.

'I'm going to test it at home tonight,' Kirk said.

After Mr Brisbane moved on, Richie turned to

Kirk. 'Maybe *I* could test it at home.'

'Have you ever sailed a model boat before?' asked Kirk.

Richie admitted that he hadn't. 'But I can tell if it sails or sinks.'

'Look, I've done this before, with my dad,' Kirk explained. 'He knows all about boats. He was in the Navy!'

'But I haven't done anything,' Richie complained.

'Lucky you,' said Kirk. 'You'll get a prize and you don't have to do the work.'

I guess Richie couldn't think of anything else to say, but he sure looked miserable.

Gail didn't look any happier. Heidi was off sick with a bad cold, so she had to work alone. And her mother, who was so encouraging to the other students, continued to insist that she decorate the sail.

'Why can't it be white?' Gail asked.

'That's so unimaginative,' Mrs Morgenstern replied. 'Be creative!'

So Gail spent a lot of time working on the hull of the boat. I think she was delaying the time when she had to decorate the sail (or upset her mum if she didn't).

I felt sorry for Richie and Gail, but at least they'd have the chance to sail on Potter's Pond and have a picnic with treasure, while I'd just sit in Room 26 with no one to talk to but a twangy old frog. I know, Og's a nice guy and I wasn't being fair to him, but I was feeling mighty low.

Even when Mrs Brisbane read from *Jolly Roger's Guide to Life*, I wasn't very cheered up.

In the evenings, I had to listen to the splishing and splashing coming from Og's tank, which only reminded me that he could swim as much as he liked, but I was forbidden to be in water. Ever.

I guess Aldo didn't know that I wouldn't be joining the class at Potter's Pond. He continued to whistle and dance the hornpipe and say things like 'Avast' and 'Me hearty', which only made me feel worse. On Thursday night, he said a very strange thing.

'I tell ye, me maties, this pirate life agrees with me!' Then he pushed his cleaning trolley out of Room 26, turned off the light and closed the door.

'Og?' I squeaked.

I could hear the faint splashing of water. 'Og? Do you think Aldo is going to be a pirate and sail away and we'll never see him again?'

'BOING-BOING-BOING-BOING!' Og responded in a very alarming way.

'I hope not either,' I answered, although I'm usually only guessing what Og is trying to say.

Aldo had left the blinds open so that the street light outside lit up Room 26 and bathed it in a soft glow. The tables were pushed together so the boats were all in a row.

'I'm taking a little walk, Og,' I suddenly announced, flinging my cage door open.

I was able to drop down from the table where Og and I live directly onto the table with the boats. It was grand seeing them up close. There was the beautiful swan boat, using real feathers that Sayeh and Miranda brought in. The pirate flag looked wonderfully menacing on the boat Garth and A.J. built. I could only admire the colourful Chinese junk that Tabitha and Seth designed. The Viking boat that Art and Mandy created tilted a bit too much to one side, but they still had time to fix it.

The tall ship was missing, because Kirk had taken it home to test it.

Gail's boat (and it was practically hers alone, since Heidi had been sick all week) was plain and simple, just like the poster of the classic sailboat on the wall.

My friends were doing a GREAT-GREAT-GREAT job and in spite of my own disappointment, I was proud of them. But I suddenly remembered the boat I'd sketched in my notebook: the S.S. *Golden Hamster* with its hamster flag. None of my friends had even thought of a flag!

I looked around at the piles of art supplies in front of me, and picked out a lovely triangle of tinfoil and a toothpick. I carefully inserted the toothpick in the foil, and what do you know? It looked like a silvery flag on a flagpole. I planted it right in front of Gail's boat, sticking it in a mound of modelling clay. It was a way to make my mark and congratulate my friends on their good work, even though they'd never know whose flag it was. After all, it wasn't their fault I'd be a landlubber for ever.

·ö·

It didn't take long for Gail to notice the flag the next morning. Heidi was back, I was happy to see, and she asked who had made it. When the girls asked around, no one knew anything about it. (*I* knew, of course, but they forgot to ask me.)

When Mrs Morgenstern came over to check on their progress, she asked Gail how she'd decided to decorate the sail.

'Mum, could I make a flag instead?' she asked.

'Good idea!' Mrs Morgenstern replied. 'So original.'

Gail went right to work. First she studied nautical flags in one of Mrs Brisbane's books. It turns out there's a whole language for flags. Boats raise them to send messages to shore or to other boats. Then Gail designed her own series of flags with brightly coloured stripes and patterns. I was happy I'd been able to inspire her and be a small part of the boat race.

Mr Brisbane drilled holes in the wood and helped her glue them in. Mrs Morgenstern loved them, and best of all, Gail did, too.

It was a fine boat. They were all fine boats, especially after Mr Brisbane helped Art and Mandy to get their Viking ship to stand up straight.

Kirk looked very pleased when Mr Brisbane checked out the tall ship.

'It floated perfectly last night,' Kirk said. 'I knew it would.'

Mr Brisbane was full of praise. After he moved on, Kirk turned to Richie and said, 'I think we've pretty much got First Prize wrapped up.'

'*You've* got First Prize wrapped up,' Richie snapped. 'I'm just a big nobody.'

Kirk looked surprised. 'Come on, Richie. No one has to know I did all the work. You'll look like a winner.'

'But I won't feel like one.' Richie quickly got up and sharpened about a million pencils. Mrs Brisbane finally noticed and went over to talk to him.

'Is everything okay?' she asked.

'I guess,' he answered.

She tried to get more information out of him, but he just kept sharpening pencils. So she wandered over to Kirk and asked him if everything was all right.

'Yeah. The boat's fantastic – look!' he answered.

'I mean between you and Richie,' Mrs Brisbane continued.

'Yeah. We make a great team,' Kirk said. He sounded as if he meant it.

'Does Kirk really think Richie doesn't mind being left out?' I squeaked to Og.

'BOING,' Og answered. He didn't sound very enthusiastic.

If ye make a fellow pirate sad and angry, ye might end up walking the plank!

from *Jolly Roger's Guide to Life* by I.C. Waters

5

Anchors Aweigh!

Richie cheered up a little when Mrs Brisbane announced that I'd be going home with him for the weekend. I was happy, too, because I didn't think he was interested in thinking about boats any more than I was. But once I got to the Rinaldi home, I found out I was WRONG-WRONG-WRONG.

There was always a lot going on at Richie's house with his parents, brothers, sisters, aunts, uncles and cousins hanging out there. It was fun, but this time Richie seemed unusually serious, despite the jokes and laughs.

On Saturday afternoon, Richie cleaned my cage. Then he unexpectedly slipped me into his pocket. It was dark in there, but I could make out a couple of dried-up raisins and half a stick of gum stuck to the cloth. Luckily, I was only in there for a few seconds.

Richie went into the bathroom, locked the door, took me out of his pocket and set me in an empty soap dish. I was a little nervous when he started filling the bathtub with water, but he said, 'Don't worry, Humphrey. You're not getting a bath. I just want to show you something.'

Once the bath was full, he showed me a strange-looking boat. 'This is my remote-controlled submarine. Pretty cool, isn't it?'

It was dark and sleek and very nice. After he put it in the bath, he used a separate remote control to make it move through the water.

'I can control when it goes up and when it goes down,' he explained. 'I'm going to take this to Potter's Pond so I can sink Kirk's ship.'

'Don't!' I squeaked. 'That's a very bad idea!'

'I don't care if it destroys the stupid thing. He thinks he's so smart, he can't lose. Well, I'll show him he can.'

'Richie. Don't. Richie. Please.' I had never felt so unsqueakably frustrated before. If only he could understand me . . . even just a little.

'It may be bad, but so is the way he's treated me,' he said, making the submarine dive to the bottom of the bathtub. 'I'll hide it in my rucksack. Then I'll move the submarine under his boat and bring it up to the top. That'll throw his stupid boat on its side.'

'It's WRONG-WRONG-WRONG!' I tried to

tell him. But it was no use.

'I'll probably get into big trouble,' Richie admitted. 'But at least he won't win.'

My mind was racing. If I could get out of my cage later, maybe I could take the batteries out of his controller. But Richie put the submarine and the remote control in a cupboard way up high. I could see there was no way a small hamster could reach it.

I've helped a lot of my friends on a lot of my weekend visits, but there was no way I could think of to help Richie.

'It'll be our little secret,' he told me.

It wasn't a secret I wanted to keep.

·ö·

'Good news, class,' Mrs Brisbane announced. 'The weather tomorrow should be picture-perfect, so the picnic at Potter's Pond is on.'

My friends gave a cheer. Even though the picnic was *off* for me, I managed a celebratory squeak.

Aldo also seemed keyed up when he cleaned the room that night. He was in and out in a hurry and when he left, he said, 'Tomorrow I set sail. Farewell, maties!'

Everyone was setting sail, except Og and me.

I'd already told Og about the submarine, but as the day went on, I thought that Richie would change his mind. He was upset, sure. I didn't blame him for that. But Richie was a good guy and good guys don't do bad things, do they?

Anyway, the boat building was over, so late that night, I decided to leave my cage and take one more look at the beautiful boats my classmates worked so hard on. They looked seaworthy enough, thanks to Mr Brisbane's advice. And they were beautiful, with Mrs Morgenstern's help. Gail's nautical flags were bright and colourful, as was the Chinese junk. But in the end, my favourite was the tall ship, because it looked as if it could sail FAR-FAR-FAR away.

Standing in front of this wonderful boat was about as close as I was going to come to the adventure I'd been wishing for. I longed to be a little bit closer. It couldn't hurt if I just crawled into the boat and pretended to sail for a minute or two, could it?

I stood at the bow of the boat and tried to imagine what it would be like to be captain of such a fine vessel.

'Ready about!' I squeaked. 'Trim the sails! Man the fo'c'sle.'

I admit, I didn't know what all those things meant, but I'd heard them in that pirate movie I'd watched.

'Lower the boom! Batten down the hatches!' It

felt good to say those things.

'Heave-ho!' I shouted. I heard Og splashing in the background, but I was hardly aware that I was in Room 26.

I don't know how long I spent pretending to be sailing. I only know that after a while, I suddenly felt sleepy. Sleepier than I've ever been, in fact. It must have been the fresh sea air I was imagining.

I turned and noticed a nice piece of sailcloth in the bottom of the boat. I decided that a short doze was in order, so I burrowed under the cloth and closed my eyes. I guess I was dreaming, because I could see the boat gliding across a silver sea, and then the dream turned SCARY-SCARY-SCARY because I saw a pirate ship approaching.

'Turn back!' I yelled. 'Trim the sails! Flibber the gibbet!'

I wasn't making much sense but it sounded pretty good. Suddenly, in my dream, a huge wave came up and shook the boat. I was being violently tossed around by the waves (and feeling slightly sick, too). And I heard the ship's bell chiming an odd sound: 'BOING-BOING-BOING!'

That's when I woke up. I pulled back the sailcloth just enough for me to see that I was moving right out of Room 26. Og had tried to warn me, but I guess the cloth muffled the sound.

I heard voices.

'Can't I carry it?' Richie begged.

'Better if I do it,' Kirk replied.

It took me a few sleepy moments to realize that I was still in the tall ship, which the boys were carrying to the bus for the trip to Potter's Pond! I was about to squeak up in protest, when I realized that, at last, I had my one chance for real adventure.

'Nice breezy day for sailing,' I heard Mr Brisbane say.

I burrowed back under the cloth. I could hear my friends chattering away and soon I felt the vibration of the bus.

'Everybody find a seat.' That, I knew, was the familiar voice of Miss Victoria, the bus driver.

Eventually, the rumbling of the bus stopped. 'All out for Potter's Pond,' Mrs Brisbane announced.

There was so much noise, so much bumping and thumping, so much confusion that all I could do was to lie low, hang on tightly and hope for the best.

'Boys and girls, on the count of three, set your boats on the water,' I heard Mrs Brisbane say.

'One . . . two . . . three!'

There was a big bump, a bigger thump and then – oh my – I felt myself floating for the first time in my life. It felt like I was riding on a cloud.

My classmates screamed, 'Go, go, go!' Once I was used to the feeling of drifting on water, I pushed the cloth back a little and peeked over the side of the boat.

What a sight! Ahead of me, rippling blue water. In the distance, a leafy green shoreline. On either side of me, my friends' boats, now afloat. Above me, sails rippling in the breeze. The ship was sailing so brilliantly, I relaxed. Richie had been upset, sure, but he would never sink this beauty.

I looked behind me just in time to see the delicate swan boat that Sayeh and Miranda had worked so hard on rapidly sink out of view. There were moans and groans and I could see my classmates were lined up on both sides of the pond to cheer their boats on.

The pirate ship was the next to go under. There were more groans, but others cheered for the remaining boats. Was my boat going to sink next? My tummy did a FLIP-FLOP-FLIP. But my tall ship seemed to glide effortlessly through the water. Kirk really did know what he was doing.

I stood up and saw that the Chinese junk and the flag-filled sailing boat were still on the water, but lagging far behind me. Even further back was the tip of the Viking ship, which was sinking rapidly. For the first time, I felt the soft breeze against my fur. It was glorious!

'Go-go-go!' my friends chanted. Then suddenly I heard Lower-Your-Voice-A.J.'s loud voice booming,

'Humphrey Dumpty's on that boat!'

There was a gasp, and Mrs Brisbane shouted, 'It *is* Humphrey! How did he get on that boat? Kirk?'

In the distance, I heard Kirk say, 'I don't know.' He sounded confused. 'I didn't see him.'

'Somebody's going to be in big trouble.' Mrs Brisbane didn't sound happy at all.

I was already in big trouble, but still, as the boat glided through the water, I felt freer than I've ever been. This was my greatest adventure yet, and I decided to enjoy it.

Pillaging and plundering can be a bit wearing, but thar be no better place to live than on the open sea!

from *Jolly Roger's Guide to Life* by I.C. Waters

All at Sea

'Ahoy, maties!' I squeaked towards shore, even though I knew no one could hear me.

Then, in my best pirate voice I added, 'Argggh!'

My friends cheered me on when suddenly the boat rocked, then rolled, and my stomach felt extremely wobbly. I was desperately trying to keep my balance when I heard screams.

The bow of the boat lurched upwards and I slid toward the stern (that's the back). It was then I remembered Richie's plan.

My friends were in a panic on shore. 'Save him! Save Humphrey!' they screamed.

As I felt the boat sinking, I recalled Mrs Brisbane's dire warning about getting wet. Besides that, I wasn't sure whether I could swim or not. Just as the boat was about to go under, I saw the periscope of Richie's submarine next to me. I leaped UP-UP-UP and grabbed hold of it. I was clinging to it for dear life when the beautiful tall ship disappeared into Potter's Pond.

I'm not sure what was happening on shore but there was a lot of noise. I heard someone call Richie's name.

'He's in the bushes!' Seth shouted. There was more commotion and I heard my name again.

'Humphrey's on the boat?' Richie sounded shocked. 'How'd that happen?'

'He's hanging onto the periscope.' That was A.J. shouting. 'Look!'

Mrs Brisbane shouted at Richie. 'Can you bring him in safely?'

'I can do it,' he answered.

No hamster ever hung onto anything as tightly as I hung onto that periscope. The water was only inches below me. I wouldn't have minded being a googly-eyed green frog with no fur at all, at least for a few minutes. But soon the submarine glided to shore. Richie and Kirk waded out to rescue me. They didn't even worry about their clothes getting wet.

Mrs Brisbane examined me and put me in a little woven basket. Golden Miranda brought me a little cup of water to drink. Nice.

'Please explain what happened, Richie,' Mrs Brisbane said in a VERY-VERY-VERY cross voice.

'I didn't know Humphrey was on board,' he said. 'How'd he get there?'

That was a question only *I* could answer. 'We'll figure that out,' Mrs Brisbane said. 'But why did you sink your own ship?'

Before Richie could answer, Kirk stepped forward and said, 'I know why. It was my fault, wasn't it, Richie?'

Richie didn't answer, so Kirk continued. 'I wanted to win and I thought the only way I could was if I did all the work. That made him mad. Right?'

Richie nodded.

'I didn't realize how mad you were until today,' Kirk said. Then he turned to Mrs Brisbane. 'If anything had happened to Humphrey, it would have been my fault, too.'

'I agree,' our teacher answered. 'So what do you have to say?'

'I'm sorry, Richie.' Kirk really sounded sorry, too. 'Winning wouldn't have been worth it, if something had happened to Humphrey.'

'I'm sorry, too.' Richie was embarrassed. 'It was a dumb idea to sink the boat. I was just so mad.'

'Boys, I'll deal with you later,' Mrs Brisbane said. 'Right now, it's time for a treasure hunt!'

My classmates and I squealed with delight when Mr Brisbane passed out treasure maps (the 'sure maps' from the list). He said, 'Boys and girls, it's said that the famous pirate, Captain Kidd, buried his treasure right here by Potter's Pond.'

So that's who Captain Ki was! Captain Kidd.

'If you follow these old maps, maybe you'll find the hidden treasure,' Mr Brisbane explained. 'Remember, X marks the spot.'

All my friends set off among the paths and trees, looking for clues. I longed to join them, but I'd had enough adventures for one day, so I watched and listened.

It wasn't too long before I heard Mandy shout, 'I found it! There's the X.' There was a rush of foot-steps. Mrs Brisbane picked up my basket and said, 'Come on, Humphrey. You might as well see this, too.'

She carried me to a little clearing where Mandy, Art and Tabitha stood by an old trunk that looked just like a pirate's treasure chest.

'Should we open it?' Tabitha asked.

Suddenly, a pirate leaped out of the bushes and said, 'Avast, maties! No one touches Captain Kidd's treasure, and them that try end up in Davy Jones's locker, asleep in the deep!'

Some of my friends screamed at the sight of the stranger, with his eyepatch, pirate hat and fear-some moustache. He lunged at the crowd. 'Land-lubbers!' he shouted. 'Scurvy dogs!'

Was this really Captain Kidd? I could swear I'd seen that moustache before.

Then Richie called out, 'It's Uncle Aldo!' and the other students started to laugh. 'It's Aldo!' they yelled.

Of course it was Aldo! He'd been practising being a pirate for two whole weeks. He gave a jolly laugh. 'Be ye ready for the treasure?' He opened the trunk. Inside were mounds of yummy sandwiches and juices and sweets.

My friends acted as if they'd never seen food before. While they ate, Aldo played a recording and danced a Sailor's Hornpipe. Everyone loved it, especially me.

'Well done, me hearty!' I squeaked, but no one could hear me over the applause.

Then Mrs Brisbane quietened everyone down. 'Don't you think it's time for the prizes?'

Everyone cheered when Sayeh and Miranda received blue ribbons. Even though their swan boat didn't last, it was the Most Beautiful Boat

But when it came to the Most Seaworthy boat, it wasn't so easy to decide who won.

'Undoubtedly, the tall ship would have won,' Mr Brisbane said. 'But because of what happened, I can only award it Honourable Mention.' Richie and Kirk didn't seem disappointed to receive red ribbons.

'As for first place, we were all so busy worrying about Humphrey, no one really noticed which boat came in first. Since Seth and Tabitha's Chinese junk and Heidi and Gail's sailing boat both made it to shore, we're calling it a tie. You'll all receive gold ribbons.'

Red, blue and gold ribbons. So that was what Mrs Brisbane wrote on her list! From the cheers and smiles I could tell that no one was disappointed.

At last, it was time to get back to school. As everyone else was busy packing up, I spotted Kirk and Richie wading way out in the water to retrieve their tall ship from the bottom of Potter's Pond. Luckily, the water only came up to their knees. When they finally pulled the boat out of the water, it was muddy and mucky but they cleaned it up, working together.

Mrs Brisbane paused near my basket. 'Humphrey, you come up with the most unusual ways to bring people together,' she told me.

'That's what a classroom hamster is for,' I replied.

That night, back in Room 26, I was almost too tired to squeak, but I managed to tell Og all about my great adventure and tried not to leave anything out.

'I have to say, Og, that as I was about to sink, I

thought of you.' It was strange to remember seeing his goofy face flash before me.

'I know if you'd been there, you would have saved me, because you can swim. And because you're my friend.'

I was surprised at how quickly Og responded with a 'BOING-BOING-BOING-BOING-BOING!'

'I'd do the same for you,' I continued. 'I can't swim, but I'd think of something. I guess we make a pretty good team after all. And so do Kirk and Richie, now.'

Og dived into the water with an impressive splash.

And with that, I crawled into my sleeping hut and slept soundly, dreaming about the high seas, pirates, best friends and the adventures yet to come.

If ye don't like danger, adventure, the open sea and lots o' gold, don't be a pirate!

from *Jolly Roger's Guide to Life* by I.C. Waters

Join me for more FUN-FUN-FUN adventures . . .

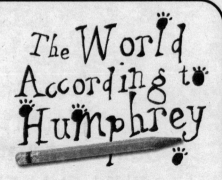

The World According to Humphrey

Dear Friends,

When I first came to live in Room 26, everybody loved me . . . except Mrs. Brisbane! Her husband wasn't exactly happy to meet me either. Find out how I won them over in my very first book of adventures.

Your friend always,
Humphrey

The World According to Humphrey

Betty G. Birney

Friendship According to Humphrey

Dear Friends,

I was green with envy when Og the Frog moved into Room 26. He had no fur at all and wasn't a bit friendly. My fellow students were all having problems with their friends, too. It took a clever hamster (me) to set things straight and a lumpy green frog to teach me the true meaning of friendship.

Your friend to the end,
Humphrey

Friendship According to Humphrey

Betty G. Birney ff

Coming soon . . .

Dear Friends,

Trouble was brewing all over Room 26. I was GLAD-GLAD-GLAD that my friends named their model town after me. But I was SAD-SAD-SAD that Golden-Miranda was in big trouble and it was all my fault! I just had to help her, even if it meant I'd be locked up forever.

Your funny, furry friend,
Humphrey

What's more fun than a computer mouse? A computer hamster – that's me! You can have FUN-FUN-FUN with me online at my brand new website:

www.funwithhumphrey.com

Ears up . . .

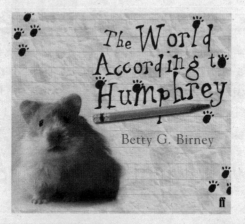

Now you can hear me squeak up for myself! Listen to *The World According to Humphrey* in audio, coming in April. And *Friendship According to Humphrey* will be published in audio in October!